This book belongs to:

....

For Pauline Lock F.S.

For Ying Liu J.L.

First published in Great Britain in 2003
by Orion Children's Books
a division of the Orion Publishing Group Ltd
Orion House
5 Upper St Martin's Lane
London WC2H 9EA

Concept, design and illustrations © James Lucas 2003
Text © Francesca Simon 2003

The right of Francesca Simon and James Lucas to be identified as the author and illustrator respectively of this work has been asserted.

A catalogue record for this book is available from the British Library.

Printed in Italy

LITTLE YELLOW DOG
GETS A SHOCK

WORDS BY FRANCESCA SIMON • PICTURES BY JAMES LUCAS

Orion
Children's Books

Little Yellow Dog trotted into
the sitting room.

WHOOPEE!

This was his lucky day.
The chair was empty.

Ginger Cat was licking her paws by the window.

'Hi, Ginger Cat,'

said Little Yellow Dog.

'Hi, Little Yellow Dog,'

said Ginger Cat.

'**Time for my nap,**' said Little Yellow Dog.

He leapt into the chair.

So did Ginger Cat.

'I got here first,'

'Hey. Off!'

said Little Yellow Dog.

said Ginger Cat.

'This chair isn't big enough for both of us,'

growled Little Yellow Dog.

'Too right. Get off,'

hissed Ginger Cat, giving
him a great big push.

'How did I end up on *the* floor?'
said Little Yellow Dog.

'**HEY!**
It's not fair.'

Little Yellow Dog had an idea.

He
crept
up
to
the
chair . . .

... sneaked behind ...

and ...

'RAAAAAA!' shrieked Little Yellow Dog

Ginger Cat went flying.

'Look out...

...it's the monster!'

Yelled Little Yellow Dog.

'And...he's...coming...

...to...get...you!'

On and on and on they ran, until they were too tired to run any more.

'Friends?'
said Little Yellow Dog.

'Friends,'
said Ginger Cat.

'We can share the chair,'
said Little Yellow Dog.

'Of course we can,'
said Ginger Cat.

But when they saw the chair,
they got a shock.

Bad Rabbit was there!

'Oi, get off our chair!'
said Little Yellow Dog and Ginger Cat.

'It's a shared chair,' said Bad Rabbit.

'Snuggle up!'